My Fox Begins

David Blaze

D1010175

For Zander...

Wow! That's Awesome!

CONTENTS

EARLY ONE MORNING

"You're not like the rest of us," a kid fox said to him. "You don't belong here." Five other kid foxes were with him. They all had bodies of brown hair with white chests and white-tipped tails. They looked like him.

He wanted to play with them. They had been kicking a pine cone around the forest, keeping it away from each other. It looked like fun. "I want to be your friend."

"Look at you," the first kid fox said. "You walk on two legs like a human." Another kid fox snickered. "And your eyes are weird.

They're bright blue. You're a freak." The other red foxes had brown, orange, yellow, or green eyes. They laughed at him.

His tail sank to the ground. He watched as the kid foxes ran off, kicking the pine cone. He'd probably never see them again, and he was glad. The forest was huge.

"Little Fox, where are you?" his mama called from their den. He didn't have a name yet, but he knew she was talking to him. The red foxes were not given names until they did something great.

He ran to the den on his two hind legs. "Here I am, Mama."

"Don't run off like that again," she scolded him. "You know it's dangerous out there." Her eyes narrowed. "Don't go out unless one of us is with you." She nodded at his dad.

"I'm sorry, Mama," he said. "I just want to be like the other kid foxes." He felt trapped in that den, like his parents were ashamed of him and didn't want the other foxes to see him.

She nudged his hand. "What other kid foxes?" His tail was still down.

"I saw them out there," he said. He pointed

outside.

"What?" his dad asked. He was a quiet fox and didn't speak much. "Did they hurt you?" Little Fox shook his head. His dad didn't trust anyone but his own family.

"They were just playing a game with a pine cone," Little Fox assured him. He looked down. "They wouldn't let me play with them."

His mama rubbed her head against his leg. "Little foxes can be mean sometimes."

"And trouble," his dad added. "Lots and lots of trouble."

Little Fox crossed his arms. "They said I walk like a human." He had no idea what a human was. He guessed it was a monster that nobody liked. If that's what a human was, then it was the right word for him.

His mama glanced at his dad. He took a deep breath and said, "Okay. It's time."

Little Fox put his arms in the air. "Time for what?"

His mama smiled. "It's time for you to learn the truth."

MID-MORNING, Part 1

Little Fox followed his dad through the forest for miles. "Keep moving!" his dad yelled at him over and over. Little Fox stopped every time he saw something new. Beautiful flying creatures surrounded them. His dad called them butterflies. Small, red creatures bit his paws. His dad called them ants. Little Fox didn't like ants.

They stopped when there were no more trees in front of them. A great wall of silver string stood in their way. "It's a fence," his dad said. "It's meant to keep us out."

"Out of what?" Little Fox wondered aloud. His dad pointed through the fence at piles of wood standing up in a perfect square. It was tall and wide. It was colored pink with blue trim.

"That's a chicken coop," his dad said. Little Fox didn't know what that meant. "It's where chickens live. Lots of them."

Little Fox's stomach growled. He loved to eat chicken! He licked his lips. So that was where chickens came from. He had always wondered how they magically appeared on his plate for dinner. He reached for the fence to climb over it.

His dad bit his tail and pulled him back. "Wait," he said. "That's not why we're here."

Little Fox threw his paws up. "Why not? We're foxes and those are chickens in there." Why had his dad taken him all the way out there? Was it a lesson to teach him not to disobey his parents again?

A loud bang came from farther beyond the fence. Little Fox jumped. It sounded like wood slamming against wood. "Lie on the ground and stay quiet," his dad told him. Little Fox hated to do it because he preferred to stand tall on his hind legs.

What he saw next took his breath away. A creature much taller than him walked on two legs toward the chicken coop. It had a soft, kind face like his mama's—but much rounder. The only hair it had was on its head, and that was gray. The top half of its body had pink cloth over it. Its legs were covered in thick blue cloth.

"What is that?" Little Fox asked his dad. It was the most amazing thing he'd ever seen.

MID-MORNING, Part 2

His dad growled softly. "That's a human." That was a human? It wasn't scary at all! Little Fox watched as the human walked to the chicken coop and opened the door with one hand. The human had a bucket in its other hand.

"Come out, my little friends," the human said in a soft voice. "It's time to eat."

Little Fox's ears perked up. He had never heard the human language, but he understood every word she said. He looked at his dad. "Did you hear that?"

His dad nodded. "Their language is ancient. There's no way for us to understand them." He shook his head. "The human may have seen us and warned the chickens."

Little Fox was confused. How could his dad not understand the human? Little Fox knew he was different than the other red foxes, but this didn't make any sense. "She's going to feed the chickens," he told his dad. "She told them to come out."

His dad huffed when dozens of chickens walked out of the coop. The human reached into her bucket and threw out grains to the chickens. They happily pecked at the grains.

Little Fox's dad stared at him. His dad probably thought he was weird, just like the little red foxes did. There had to be something wrong with him.

"Good morning, Rita," a different human voice said. Fox looked up to see the human kneeling in front of a chicken. "It's a beautiful day," the chicken said.

Little Fox choked. The chicken spoke

human! He stared at it with big eyes and saw the chicken had the same bright blue eyes as him. He couldn't believe it!

"Yes, it is a beautiful day, Old Nelly," the human said. She looked up into the sky. "Looks like we might get rain later." She nodded at the chicken. "It will be good for the grass. It could be greener."

"Did you hear that?" Little Fox asked his dad. "Old Nelly speaks like a human!" His dad continued to stare at him.

"We need to go," his dad said. "It's not safe here."

Little Fox did not want to leave. They weren't in any danger—he was sure of it. "I can talk to the human. I can ask her to be our friend."

"NEVER talk to humans," his dad said in a deep voice that scared him. "They cannot be trusted." He stood slowly and quietly on four paws. "I don't want to hear another word about it. Let's go."

"But—" Little Fox said.

"NOW," his dad commanded.

Little Fox looked back at Rita and Old Nelly. They talked and laughed like they were best friends. He wanted to be a part of that. Maybe this was the one place he would be accepted.

He walked away quietly on four paws with his dad. Little Fox only stopped when another red ant bit his paw. Red ants were mean! He couldn't stop thinking about Rita and Old Nelly. One day he'd find a way to talk to them.

LATE MORNING, PART 1

"He can understand the humans," Little Fox's dad told his mama. They were in the den and sitting in a circle. "I was afraid of this."

"The human is like you, Mama," Little Fox said. "She's nice and pretty." Sure, the human looked different than them, but she wasn't scary.

His mama stroked his head. "You are special, Little Fox. You're going to do great things."

His dad stood on four paws and huffed.

"He's going to put us in danger." He walked in circles around the room. "He must not be allowed to talk to the humans." His face was like stone, and his voice was deep again. Little Fox shivered. "We are red foxes!"

His mama stood. "Little Fox, go outside and play. Don't go far. Make sure I can see you." She stared at him until he stood. "I need to talk to your dad."

Little Fox watched as his dad continued to walk in a circle. His chest heaved up and down. Little Fox had never seen him so angry. He listened to his mama and ran out of the den.

"What happened today doesn't change anything," he heard his mama say back in the den. "He's still a fox. And he's still our son."

Little Fox didn't hear his dad say anything. He imagined his dad was still walking in circles and shaking his head. He didn't understand why his dad was so angry about this. There wasn't any reason why red foxes and humans couldn't be friends.

Little Fox jumped when he heard a rustle to his right. He looked over and saw a strange animal, smaller than him, looking at him. It was black with a white chest, a white streak of hair down its back, and a head full of white hair. It also had bright blue eyes!

Little Fox looked into the den and saw his parents weren't watching him. His dad was walking in circles and his mama was trying to calm him down. Little Fox knew he had to meet the strange animal. He could step away for a minute.

"Hi," Little Fox said to the animal in the human language. He had never spoken it before, but it was easy. He suspected the animal with blue eyes could understand him. "I want to be your friend."

LATE MORNING, PART 2

"Hi!" the animal said to him. He sounded like a kid. He stood on his hind legs just like Little Fox and waved. "I'm Stinky the skunk. Sure, we can be friends."

Little Fox smiled. Stinky was his first friend! "You can call me Little Fox." He wondered why his new friend was called Stinky. "How did you get your name?"

"It's a joke," Stinky said. "The other skunks call me that to make fun of me." He shrugged his shoulders. "Skunks are supposed to stink," he continued. "When we're scared or in danger, we spray a stinky liquid at our enemies." He laughed. "It sticks to them, and they can't get the smell off for a long time."

Little Fox wondered what it smelled like. "Does it smell like farts?"

Stinky laughed. "It's worse than that. You can't wash the smell off of you. It's disgusting."

Little Fox wasn't sure it could be worse. "One time, my dad asked me to pull his finger." He shuddered when he recalled the nightmare. "I wasn't sure why he asked, but he farted when I pulled his finger."

Stinky's mouth was wide open like he was amazed. "Your dad is my hero."

One thing didn't make sense to Little Fox. He put his paws in the air. "If skunks are supposed to stink, then why is your name a joke?"

Stinky shrugged. "I can't spray my enemies like the other skunks. When I get scared or nervous, I run away." He looked down at the ground. "The other skunks don't like me. I hope we can still be friends."

Little Fox put a hand on Stinky's shoulder.

"Of course we're friends!" They were both different. They were the only animals he knew of that could walk upright and speak human. Stinky and Little Fox were connected somehow.

"Get out of here, skunk!" Little Fox's dad shouted from behind him. He bared his teeth and growled. Stinky didn't speak the red fox language, but the sharp teeth and deep growl explained everything.

The hair on Stinky's head stood straight up. He turned around and ran away faster than a streak of lightning.

"Dad!" Little Fox shouted. "That was my new friend!"

"Your mama told you to stay near the den," his dad said. "You don't listen, and that's going to get you into trouble one day." He shook his head. "Come with me."

Fox looked through the woods to see if he could spot Stinky. As fast as the skunk ran off, he was a mile away by then. Had Little Fox lost the only friend he ever had? He sighed. "Where are we going?" he asked.

His dad walked past him. "We're going back

to the chicken coop."

EARLY AFTERNOON

Little Fox stood tall on two legs with his dad next to him in front of the silver fence again. The chicken coop was closed, and the chickens were inside. His dad hadn't said a word on the trip there. "Do you want me to talk to the human?" Little Fox asked.

His dad grunted. "Forget about the human. We're going to hunt."

Little Fox had never hunted before. He thought about Old Nelly. Nothing could happen to the chicken. She was like him. "I'm not hungry," he said. His stomach growled.

His dad looked up at him. "I won't always be able to take care of you. I need to know that you can take care of yourself."

Little Fox gulped. His dad had never talked to him like that. Little Fox couldn't imagine his life without him. He wanted to prove to his dad that he wasn't so little anymore. "What do I have to do?"

His dad nodded. "I've been watching this place for weeks. The human sleeps in the afternoon." He motioned to the chicken coop. "I want you to catch one of those chickens."

Little Fox cocked his head. "Me? Aren't you going to help?"

His dad shook his head. "You can do this. I know you can."

Little Fox gulped. He jumped up and grabbed the top of the fence. He pulled himself over and fell flat on his back on the other side. It hurt more than the red ant bites. His dad appeared upside down. "I'm okay," Little Fox said.

He turned over and stood on four paws so he could move with stealth. When he got to the chicken coop, he used his paws to unlatch the door. It creaked open.

Little Fox stood up on his two hind legs. Inside the coop were chickens on the right and on the left. Some were up high on shelves and some were down low. They were everywhere. Jackpot!

"Rita!" Old Nelly yelled. "Help! Fox!"

The chickens went crazy. They screamed, "Kuh-kuh-kuh-KACK!"

The loud bang of wood against wood came from farther in the yard. The ground shook as Rita's footsteps raced toward the coop. Little Fox got down on four legs and turned to see her pointing a long, skinny wooden object at him. "Oh no, you don't!" she shouted at him. "Get away from my chickens!"

Little Fox couldn't move. His chest pounded hard. His heart felt like it was going to explode. His legs shook.

Rita stepped closer to him. "You're scared,

aren't you?" She lowered the long wooden object. "You're just a kid, a fox cub."

Little Fox wanted to tell her, "Yes," but he remembered what his dad had said. *NEVER talk to humans.* But was he right about humans being dangerous?

"You have beautiful blue eyes," Rita said. She patted his head. "You can understand me, can't you?"

Little Fox was happy she already knew. He was about to say, "Yes," when his dad raced up behind Rita. His dad bared his sharp teeth and growled at her. She dropped her gun and fell to the ground.

"Let's go!" his dad shouted to him. "Now!"

Little Fox looked at Rita. She nodded at him. "It's okay," she said. "Come back and see me when you're older. I have much to tell you."

Little Fox winked at her and ran off with his dad.

MID-AFTERNOON

"What happened?" his mama asked when they got back to the den. She was making up the beds.

"It didn't go as planned," his dad said. "But Little Fox was brave. I'm proud of him. He stared danger in the face."

Little Fox was happy his dad was proud of him. But he didn't want his dad to think he was in danger. "Rita—the human—wouldn't have hurt me. She wants to help."

"There you go with that nonsense again," his dad said. They were both on four paws. His dad put his face right in front of his. "She wants to help? She pointed a gun at you."

"What?" his mama said. "You let a human point a gun at my baby?"

"Not now, dear," his dad said. "Listen to me, Little Fox. Guns are used to hunt red foxes. Humans hunt us the same way we hunt chickens." His voice got deep again. "That human is not your friend. She cannot be trusted."

"But—" Little Fox said.

"You need to take a nap," his dad said. "It's been a long day. Go lie down."

Little Fox looked to his mama for support. She shrugged her shoulders like there was nothing she could do. "You never listen to me," he said to his dad before he stomped to his bed.

His mama tucked him into his bed. "I know it's hard to see it sometimes, but your dad just wants what's best for you. He loves you more than you will ever know."

Little Fox wasn't sure about that. His dad thought he was weird like the other red foxes did. At least that's what Little Fox believed.

He yawned. He wondered what it would be like to talk to Rita. She had the answers to why he was the way he was. Why was he so much like a human?

He fell asleep and dreamed of chasing chickens. Only, he didn't hunt them. He played with them.

LATE AFTERNOON

"Wake up, Little Fox," his mama said. "It's almost dinner time."

He yawned and stretched his paws. It was fun playing with the chickens in his dreams. "What are we eating?" he asked.

She patted his head. "Your dad is out looking for food." Little Fox knew his dad wouldn't go back to the chicken coop. They'd eat what they did most days—crickets, caterpillars, beetles or grasshoppers.

"Go wash up in the river," his mom continued. "We don't want your grubby paws all over the food." He looked at his paws. They were black with dirt and mud.

"Really?" he asked. He had never been allowed to go to the river by himself. It wasn't far away. His dad had built the den years ago so they would be close to water. "What will Dad say?"

She kissed his cheek. "Don't worry about your dad. I'll take care of him."

Little Fox jumped out of bed and headed for the den exit. "I'm going now…" He waited for his mama to stop him. "I'm stepping outside…" She had to be kidding about letting him go to the river. "I'm going to the river—"

"Bye, Little Fox," his mama said. "Come right back when you're done."

Little Fox shrugged and raced out of the den before she changed her mind. He ran to the river on four paws. He was much faster that way than on two paws. *Stealth mode,* he thought. *I'm super-fast!*

He stopped at the river and stared at his reflection in the water. "You look like the other foxes," he said to his reflection. "Why do you have to be so different?" His mama had told him that he was born with green eyes and took his first steps with four paws. His eyes turned blue the first time he stepped out of the den and into the forest. He stood and walked on two legs that same day. The land had changed him.

Little Fox turned and fell into the water when another reflection appeared next to his. Looking closer, he noticed it was his friend Stinky the skunk!

"Don't worry," Stinky said. "I'm the cleanest skunk around." He smiled and laughed.

Little Fox climbed out of the water and shook his body dry. He remembered Stinky wasn't like the other skunks. "It's no fun being different, is it?"

Stinky shrugged. "My mom says it's okay to be different. I don't have to be like the other skunks." He dipped a paw into the water. "Besides, when the right time comes, I'll find a way to stop my enemies if I have to."

Little Fox chuckled and splashed water on Stinky. "You better never spray me!"

Stinky splashed water back on Little Fox.

"You better never pull your dad's finger around me!" They laughed and jumped into the water, splashing it all over each other.

EARLY EVENING, Part 1

Little Fox's dad was waiting for him outside the den when he got back. "Come with me," his dad said. He walked into the forest without looking back. Little Fox was scared that he was in trouble.

They walked for miles in a direction Little Fox had never been. The sun was getting lower. All four of his legs were sore. He was sure his dad was punishing him. "I'm sorry, Dad," he said.

"Shh…" his dad said. He stopped walking. "Listen." Soft chirps filled the air

around them like a chorus. "Those are crickets."
Little Fox turned in circles. It sounded like the
crickets were everywhere. "I found this place
earlier," his dad continued. "I want you to help
me catch the crickets for dinner."

Little Fox stood on his hind legs and
scratched his head. If his dad was here earlier,
then why didn't he get the crickets himself?
"You want me to help you?"

His dad looked up at him. "This is what red
foxes do." He took a deep breath. His face
softened. "You're my son. You're smart and
you're fast. I can't do the things you can. What I
can do is protect you and show you how to
survive."

Little Fox nodded. His dad hadn't spoken
this way to him before. He had always been a
stern dad and never complimented him.

A loud bang filled the air. It was like wood
hitting against the wood at Rita's place but
louder. The crickets became silent. The dirt
between Little Fox and his dad jumped up and
stung them.

"Fox hunters!" his dad yelled. "Run!"

Little Fox couldn't move. He was more scared than when Rita stood over him. They were surrounded by trees. He couldn't see hunters anywhere. His legs shook again.

His dad bit his leg. Little Fox fell to four paws. "Run home to your mama," his dad said quickly. "You're faster than me. Warn her." Little Fox knew he had to keep his mama safe. "Don't look back. I'm right behind you."

Two humans walked toward them. They had long guns like Rita's in their hands. "Run!" his dad shouted again.

Little Fox took off as fast as he could. He hoped his dad could keep up with him. They had to protect his mama. He knew he wasn't supposed to look back, but he wanted to make sure his dad could keep up.

Little Fox slowed down. His dad wasn't with him. His dad had run in the opposite direction. He was running straight for the hunters.

BANG!

Little Fox turned toward his home and ran as fast as he could. "Mama!" he shouted over and over. "Mama! Mama! Mama!"

EARLY EVENING, PART 2

The trip to the land of crickets had taken hours, but Little Fox was back at the den in minutes. His mama stood outside with a worried look on her face. "Where's your dad?"

Little Fox could only think of one word. "Hunters." He focused on his mama's eyes. "He tried to stop them!" Little Fox cried. "He was supposed to be right behind me. He's supposed to be here."

His mama rubbed her head against his. "Okay," she said. Her voice was weak, like she was exhausted. "Okay, okay, okay." She looked back at the den and shook her head. She cleared her throat. "We need to get to the river." Her voice was stronger than ever. "They can't follow our tracks in the water."

Little Fox took a deep breath. "What about Dad?"

She shook her head at him. "He's not coming back."

They jumped when a large animal ran out of the trees toward them. "Dad!" Little Fox shouted. "I knew it! I knew you'd make it!"

His dad collapsed in front of them. "They're coming," he said, out of breath. "I slowed them down as much as I could."

Little Fox's mama examined his dad's leg. It had been shot. "We've got to get to the river," she said again. "It's our only chance."

"There's not enough time," his dad said. "There's only one thing we can do." He whispered something into her ear. She stared at Little Fox and nodded her head.

"Let's get back into the den," she told Little Fox. "We'll have to hide in there." He didn't question it. She always knew what was best. They'd hide in there until the hunters went away. "Hurry, go. There's no time to waste."

Little Fox jumped into the den and waited for them. The hunters would never find them there. It would all be okay.

He coughed when dirt and mud hit his face. He looked up into the den opening. It was a hole in the ground that led to their underground house. His parents were standing over it and pushing the dirt and mud and rocks inside. "What are you doing?"

"It was always supposed to be you," his mama said. She kept pushing more dirt into the hole. "You're the greatest thing that's ever happened to us."

Little Fox couldn't stop coughing. "Let me out!" he shouted. He realized they were blocking him in so the hunters couldn't see him. "Mama, please don't leave me." She didn't say anything; she just kept pushing more dirt in.

"Dad, you don't have to do this!" His dad stopped filling the hole for a moment. "My son, I believe in you. I always did. Unite the humans and the red foxes." With that, he pushed in a larger rock. The hole was completely blocked. The den was as dark as a night without a moon or stars.

"Let me out!" Little Fox shouted. "I can help!"

BANG! BANG!

"No!"

EARLY EVENING, PART 3

Little Fox froze. He listened for his parents, but they didn't say anything else. All he heard was the footsteps of humans.

"We hit them both, Billy," one of them said. "They won't make it far."

"Well, well, well… What do we have here, John?" He stomped on the ground above Little Fox. "I believe we have a foxhole."

"Looks like it's covered up," John said. "I reckon they were hiding something." He stomped on the ground too. "Maybe other foxes."

Little Fox's heart raced. His parents were gone and now the hunters would find him. He was trapped in the den. There was nowhere for him to run.

"Forget about it," Billy said. "If there are foxes in there, they'll never get out."

"That's not the point," John argued. "The Boss is paying us a lot of money to wipe out all the animals in this forest. I'm going to get every cent I can."

"Wait a second," John said. "Is that a skunk?" They both jumped. "Why is it walking toward us?"

Little Fox perked his ears up and listened for smaller footsteps. Was that Stinky? He wanted to tell his friend to run.

"Maybe it's not a foxhole," Billy said. "Maybe it's a skunk hole."

"I doubt it," John said. "They usually live in tree hollows or logs."

"More money for us," Billy said. "Do you want to shoot it or should I?"

Little Fox heard Stinky on the ground above him. The skunk stopped there and faced the hunters. Why didn't he run?

"He's cute," John said. "Not smart though.

He's just sitting there. Poor guy." Little Fox heard a clicking sound. "I've got it."

What was Stinky doing? He needed to run like he always did! Little Fox felt the ground shift. Was Stinky turning around to run away? Good! *Run, Stinky! Run!*

Little Fox heard a gushing sound, like the river.

"Nooooo!" John shouted. "He sprayed me in the eyes! Get it out! Get it out of my eyes!"

"It's all over me!" Billy screamed like a girl fox. "It smells so bad! I can't breathe!"

Yes! Little Fox thought. *He did it. Stinky did it.*

The ground vibrated when Stinky ran off. "Get him!" John shouted. "Get that skunk!" The footsteps were heavy on the ground above Little Fox as the hunters ran after Stinky.

Little Fox laid his head down in the darkness and whined. His parents were gone. Stinky was in danger. And someone named The Boss wanted to wipe out all the animals in the forest.

MID-EVENING

Little Fox stood and felt for the dirt and rocks in front of him. His parents were out there somewhere. The hunters had shot them, but his mama and dad were fighters and wouldn't give up easily. They would have gone to the river.

He put one paw in front of the other and scratched at the dirt to pull it away. It was easy until he hit rocks. It was harder to dig them out. He carried them deeper into the den so they weren't in the way.

The more he dug the more dirt and rocks

he found. It didn't seem like it would ever end. There still wasn't any light.

Little Fox was exhausted. He lay down again to rest. He had no idea if it was day or night. When he woke up, he dug again and carried rocks until he was exhausted. He was fast, but he wasn't strong like his dad.

Time disappeared. He would dig, carry rocks, dig some more, and carry more rocks. Then he would sleep for hours or days, he wasn't sure. Every now and then he'd find a cricket or worm in the dirt. The worms were disgusting. They were slimy. But he was starving. He had to eat them.

Dig. Carry rocks. Dig. Carry rocks.

Light! There was light! Little Fox dug faster. More and more light came through the hole. He could feel the wind. He was almost out!

One big rock was in the way now. It covered half of the hole. It was too heavy for him to move it. Little Fox was determined. He couldn't let his parents down. He reached through the half hole and tried to pull himself out. He sucked in his chest and squeezed through the hole.

Freedom! The sun shined bright. It had to be the afternoon. Little Fox ran on four paws to the river. "Mama! Dad! Mama! Dad!"

He ran up and down the river, shouting their names. They didn't answer. Little Fox stared at his reflection in the water. He hit the water as hard as he could to make the reflection disappear.

He went back to the den. The sun was low. He squeezed into the den and waited. He did the same thing day after day. He searched the forest for his parents. He went to the land of crickets so he could eat. He taught himself how to catch crayfish in the river. He learned to survive on his own—like his dad had taught him.

The hunters didn't return. He couldn't find his parents or Stinky anywhere, but he wouldn't stop looking. Days, weeks, and months passed. Then, one day, he realized his parents weren't coming back. There was only one thing left for him to do.

Rita, he thought. *I've got to talk to Rita. She'll*

have the answers.

A NEW DAY

Little Fox stared through the silver fence at the chicken coop. It was closed. The sun was bright. Rita would be out soon. He smiled when he heard wood slamming against wood. She was coming.

But wait. There was a different human this time. He was shorter than Rita. He appeared to be a kid. He wore black cloth with orange beneath it. Where did he come from? Where was Rita?

The kid opened the chicken coop and stepped inside. Little Fox wasn't sure what to do. He needed to talk to Rita, but this other human was there. Could this human have the same answers? Little Fox sighed. There was one way to find out. He jumped over the fence.

The kid froze when he came out of the chicken coop. He stared at Little Fox. Little Fox stared back. He stood on all four legs—he didn't want to scare the kid. He smiled.

The kid picked up a stick. Little Fox prepared to run. He didn't want to be hit by a stick. The kid threw the stick into the grass and shouted, "Fetch!"

Little Fox understood the human language, but he wasn't sure what that word meant. He figured it meant "get away". He couldn't give up now. He needed answers. Little Fox shook his head no.

"What are you?" the kid asked. "You're not a dog. If you were, then you'd have a collar." He walked toward Little Fox. He held his hands out for some reason. "This is nuts," the kid continued. "You've got to be some kind of dog. Where's your collar?"

The kid stopped right in front of him. He stared into Little Fox's eyes like he was amazed by them. Little Fox wondered if humans wore collars. He stood on his two hind legs. "I don't know," he said in his human voice. "Where's *your* collar?"

The kid fell backward and scooted away from Little Fox. It was too soon to talk to the human. Little Fox wished he had waited for Rita.

"Jonah!" another human shouted from the yard. She sounded like Rita but younger. "Where are you? You better not be in the outhouse!"

The kid sat on the ground and stared at Little Fox. He looked as scared as Little Fox felt when Rita had pointed the gun at him. Little Fox would have to fix this later. The other human could be coming.

Little Fox walked on his hind legs to the kid. "I'm a fox," he said. "Don't tell anyone you

46

saw me here." He winked at the kid to show him that he wasn't dangerous. Then Little Fox ran to the fence and jumped over it. He'd have to figure out what to do later. Maybe the kid could give him the answers he needed. And maybe, just maybe, the kid could be his friend.

Read the entire award-winning My Fox series:

DAVID BLAZE

DAVID BLAZE

DAVID BLAZE

DAVID BLAZE

DAVID BLAZE

You can keep up with everything I'm doing at:

www.davidblazebooks.com

Be sure to click the Follow button next to my name (David Blaze) on Amazon.com to be notified when my new books are released.

And you can follow me on Facebook. Just search for David Blaze, Children's Author. Be sure to like the page!

If you enjoyed my story, please tell your friends and family. I'd also appreciate it if you'd leave a review on Amazon.com and tell me what you think about my best friend, Fox.

See you soon!

Made in the USA
Las Vegas, NV
27 October 2021